WEEKENDS with MAX and His DAD

Weekends with Max and His Dad

LINDA URBAN

ILLUSTRATED BY
KATIE KATH

HOUGHTON
MIFFLIN
HARCOURT

Boston New York

hmhco.com

The text was set in 14 pt. Chaparral Pro.
Design by Christine Kettner

The Library of Congress has cataloged
the hardcover edition as follows:
Urban, Linda. Weekends with Max and his dad /
written by Linda Urban; illustrated by Katie Kath.
pages cm
Summary: Third-grader Max pursues neighborhood adventures
with his dad as they both adjust to recent changes in their family.
[1. Fathers and sons—Fiction. 2. Neighborhoods—Fiction.
3. Divorce—Fiction.] I. Kath, Katie, illustrator. II. Title.
PZ7.U637W44 2016
[Fic]—dc23
2015014878

ISBN: 978-0-544-59817-1 hardcover
ISBN: 978-1-328-90019-7 paperback

Printed in the United States
DOC 10 9 8 7 6 5 4 3 2 1
4500701886

For the

Agents Thompson

Spies

When Max's dad came to pick him up on Friday night, he said, "Tomorrow, I will show you my new neighborhood."

"Sorry, Dad," said Max. "Tomorrow I have spy duty. You'll have to call me Agent Pepperoni."

"Oh," said Dad. "Okay."

"But you can be my helper spy," said Max. "You can be Agent Cheese."

"Not Agent Lightning? Or Agent Super-Cool Guy?" asked Dad.

1

"Agent Cheese," said Max.

Max had it all planned out. He had been reading *The Sneaky Book of Spy Skills* and had been waiting until the weekend to try what he had learned. As they drove from the house Max lived in with Mom to his dad's new apartment, Max imagined himself sneaking through dark shadows and collecting top-secret information. He imagined Dad sneaking alongside him. Dad would not be wise in the ways of spies like he was, but Max didn't mind. He would tell Dad what to do.

When Dad opened the door, the new apartment was dark. He flicked on the lights. "What do you think?"

"It is very clean," said Max. He thought that sounded nicer than saying it was very white. The kitchen had a white counter and white tile floor and a white breakfast bar between it and the living room. The living room was white too, except for a black TV and an orange armchair Max

recognized from Grandma's house. The rest of
the room was empty. Max thought it would be
perfect for practicing spy moves like leaping
into action and falling from tall buildings. "I
like it," said Max.

"I haven't had much time to unpack," said Dad.

He showed Max a white bedroom with white walls and lots of cardboard boxes and a mattress on the floor. "This is my room," said Dad. "And this is the bathroom." The bathroom was white too, but there were two pale-green towels hanging on hooks and two very new-looking toothbrushes on the white countertop.

Max opened a door under the sink. There was nothing in the cupboard. *A good place for hiding,* he thought. "I like this, too," he said.

"Would you like to see your room?" asked Dad.

Max expected another white room with cardboard boxes, but when Dad opened the door, that is not what he saw. He saw a room with blue walls and a bed with a silver blanket. There was a blue dresser and football-print curtains and a lamp with a Detroit Lions football helmet for a base. And two framed photographs: one of Max and Mom at Cedar Point Amusement Park and one of Max and Dad at a football game.

"Do you like it?" asked Dad.

"It's very blue," said Max. He didn't want to say what he was really feeling. What he was feeling was like somebody was sitting on his chest. Max had liked the Detroit Lions last year, when he was in second grade. He still liked the Detroit Lions now, but not as much. And he did not think he liked blue very much at all. He could not imagine a spy with a blue room and football curtains.

"Are you okay?" asked Dad.

Max did not want to hurt Dad's feelings. "I'm tired," he said. He pretended to yawn.

Max brushed his teeth with one of the new toothbrushes in the new bathroom. Dad said there were new pajamas in his new dresser, but Max put on the soft old ones from his big weekend bag. He got out *The Sneaky Book of Spy Skills* and got into his new bed.

"All set, sport?" asked Dad.

"I'm not a sport," said Max. "I am a spy."

"That's right," said Dad. "You are Agent Pepperoni and I am Agent Flash."

"Agent Cheese," said Max.

Dad grinned. "Thought I could sneak that past you."

"You can't sneak things past a spy," said Max.

"So I see." Dad tilted the book in Max's hands so he could read the title. "Does this book say what a helper spy does?"

"A helper spy does what the main spy tells him

to. He jots down notes. He takes pictures. He is on lookout," said Max.

"Sounds good," said Dad. "When do we start?"

"Tomorrow," said Max. "First thing."

"Then we'd better get some shuteye." Dad kissed Max on the forehead. He tucked the silver covers under Max's chin. He pulled shut the football curtains and turned off the helmet lamp. "Good night, pal."

Gray light filtered through the space between the football curtains and made shadows on the walls. Max heard a thump and a rumble that were probably the heat turning on.

Probably.

There were footsteps overhead and a *clicketa-clicketa-clicketa* sound. There was a clank and a whoosh and voices. Max knew that these sounds were probably other people in other apartments.

Probably.

But Max was a spy. He knew the sounds could be other things. Dangerous things.

"Agent Cheese?" called Max.

Dad appeared in the doorway. "Yes, Agent Pepperoni?"

"You don't have to wait until tomorrow if you want. You can be on lookout now."

"You got it." Dad saluted.

Saluting was for the army, not for spies, Max knew, but he could tell Dad that tomorrow. Tonight Agent Cheese was on lookout, and that was good enough.

In the morning, Max put on his jacket with many pockets and his black spy hat and his dark spy glasses and an old necktie he had found in the basement of the house he lived in with Mom. Then he went out into the living room. Dad was sitting in the orange armchair, reading *The Sneaky Book of Spy Skills*.

"*Ahem*," said Max.

"Excuse me, sir," said Dad. "Have you seen my son? Short boy? Curly hair? Good looking,

11

like his father?"

Max laughed and took off his glasses.

"Max!" said Dad. "It's you!"

"You knew it was me," said Max.

"I kind of did," said Dad. "But that's because I know you very well. Otherwise, I would not have recognized you."

"Spies need good disguises," said Max.

"I guess I will need a disguise, then," said Dad. "Any ideas?"

Max had a bag full of ideas. He had another pair of glasses and a stick-on mustache and a bandanna. He even had a fake scar left over from his Halloween costume. He put them all on Dad, then led him to the bathroom mirror.

"This disguise is so good even I don't know who I am," said Dad.

"That's okay." Max patted Dad's elbow. "I will remind you."

"Thanks, pal." Dad smiled and his mustache fell off.

"You can't smile, Agent Cheese. You need to remain inconspicuous."

"Inconspicuous, eh?" Dad was careful not to smile with his mouth, but his eyes smiled anyway.

"It means you need to sneak around unnoticed, which you can't do if your mustache is always flying off."

"Got it," said Dad. "Oh, I almost forgot. This came while you were getting dressed."

Dad handed Max an envelope addressed to Agent Pepperoni. The words TOP SECRET were printed across the back. Max opened the envelope and read the note inside:

YOUR MISSION: FIND COFFEE

* * *

Ace's Coffee Shop was just around the corner from Dad's new apartment. It had cushy red booths to sit in, and on the walls were advertisements for old-timey things like fountain pens and shaving equipment. A painted sign hung over the cash register: COUNTY'S BEST BACON AND PINEAPPLE PANCAKES.

"Let's sit at the counter," said Dad.

Max climbed onto a red cushioned stool, and Dad sat beside him.

"I'm sorry," said a burly man in a white apron. "These seats are saved for my friend Leo. He's bringing his son, Max, here today."

Max pulled his hat down low on his forehead. "We will move when they get here," he said in a very deep voice.

"Deal," said the man, setting two menus on the counter. "I'll be right back with some coffee."

When the man turned around, Dad whispered to Max, "That's Ace. Do you think we should have told him who we really are?"

Max shook his head. "A spy never tells his secrets."

"Never?" asked Dad.

"Never," said Max. "Except to a helper spy."

"But what if there are no helper spies around?" asked Dad.

"He waits, even if it takes a whole week."

"That must be hard to do," said Dad.

"Sometimes," admitted Max.

Max picked up a menu and spun around on his stool. He held the menu just high enough to peek over as he studied the people in the restaurant. There were tall people and short people and people tapping on phones and people reading books. There was a lady with lots of tiny braids and a man with no hair at all. Two men in the corner played chess, and a woman in a booth did a crossword puzzle. She wore white nurse's shoes, like Mom did for work.

Max noticed nothing suspicious—except that none of the people in the restaurant were eating

pancakes. Puzzling. Why wouldn't people order pancakes if they were the County's Best?

Ace set a cup of coffee on the counter for Dad. "You look like a hot-chocolate man to me," he said, sliding a mug in front of Max. "So, gentlemen, what'll it be?"

"The usual," said Dad.

Max elbowed Dad. "He's joking," said Max in his very deep voice. "We have never been here before. And we will never be here again."

"Right." Dad held his mustache on and pretended to laugh at his joke. "I will have the scrambled eggs with spinach and tomato."

"And I will have the County's Best Bacon and Pineapple Pancakes," said Max.

A huge grin spread across Ace's face.

"Oh, boy," said Dad.

Ace reached under the counter and pulled out a bright red ukulele. He strummed. Everyone in the restaurant stopped what they were doing and looked right at Max. Then Ace began to sing:

"Pancakes, oh pancakes,
oh pancakes divine.
Better with bacon,
much better with
pine . . . apple.
Best in the county,
best we can make 'em.
Best with pineapple,
and bester with bac-om."

Everyone in the restaurant applauded, and Dad's mustache fell off into his coffee. Max pulled his hat down even lower. This was no way to stay inconspicuous.

But he had to admit, it was a great way to have breakfast.

In between bites of bacon-and-pineapple pancake, Max gave Dad a crash course in basic spying. He started by taking a small camera, a spiral notebook, and a pencil out of his pockets.

"I'm going to notice things," Max said, handing Dad the notebook and pencil. "And you can write down what I say."

"Ten-four, Agent Pepperoni," said Dad. "Ten-four" was a police way of saying okay, not a spy way, but Max did not say anything. He did not want Dad to get discouraged on his first day as a helper spy.

They listened as a lady in a purple turban told Ace about her basset hounds, Barkis and Peggoty. "Jot that down," said Max. "It might be important."

"Really?" asked Dad.

"Trust me," said Max. "I am a listening expert." He handed Dad the camera. "We should take some pictures, too."

Dad aimed the camera at a man eating an omelet. The man scowled.

"Try it sneaky-spy style, Agent Cheese." Max set the camera on the counter. He turned the lens to the left and—without looking at the screen—snapped two shots. *Snap snap!* He turned it to the right and did the same. *Snap snap!* Then he aimed the camera straight at his chest. "When I lean over, press the button," he whispered to Dad.

Max leaned over and pretended to tighten his shoelace. *Snap snap snap.*

"Does this really work?" asked Dad.

"Trust me," said Max. "I'm a sneaky-photo expert."

Ace put a slip of paper on the counter. "I guess my pal Leo forgot to come today," he said. "I hope he doesn't forget that the Ukulele Union meets on Wednesday night."

"I'm sure he'll remember," said Dad.

Max studied the writing on the slip of paper. There were numbers and letters on it, but the scribbly cursive was hard to read. "I am a secret-code expert," said Max, when Ace had gone to fill someone else's coffee cup. "But this message is a stumper."

"I can read it," said Dad. He took out his wallet. "I am an expert at some things too."

Just then, a man in a yellow T-shirt entered the restaurant. He had a phone in his hand and an uncomfortable look on his face. The man looked all around the room, then turned and walked out.

Finally. Something suspicious.

"Let's go, Agent Cheese," said Max.

Dad followed Max out of Ace's Coffee Shop. "Where are we going?" he asked.

"Shhh," said Max. He pointed at the man in the yellow shirt, walking just a few yards ahead of them. "Write down *yellow shirt*."

Dad wrote down *yellow shirt*.

The man stopped walking. Max and Dad stopped walking.

"Turn around," whispered Max. He and Dad turned their backs to the man. Max pulled a small mirror out of one of his many pockets and held it so that he could watch the man behind them. "He's going into that shop. Write down the name of that shop."

Dad wrote *Doctor Spin* in the notebook. "It's a music store," said Dad. "They sell real records, like in the old days. Some nights they have concerts."

"That's important background information," said Max. "Fine work, Agent Cheese."

A minute later, the man in the yellow T-shirt came out of the shop. He still had his phone in his hand, and he hadn't bought any records.

"Very suspicious," said Max.

The man continued up Birch Street. Max and Dad followed, careful to walk far enough behind that they would not be noticed.

The man went inside the Black Dog Bookstore and came back out. He went into Give It Another Go Vintage Clothing and came back out. He stopped at Museum of Shoes and Lickety Split Ice Cream and the Rialto Movie House and Jinger's Nail Salon. Every time the man in the yellow shirt went into a shop, Dad gave Max background information about the place. And every time the man came back outside, Max and Dad followed him.

The man looked around again. Max ducked behind a mailbox. Dad followed.

"Very, very suspicious," said Max. "Are you writing this all down, Agent Cheese?"

"I'm drawing a map," said Dad, handing the note-book to Max. The map was of Birch Street and of all the stores the man in the yellow shirt had stepped inside. Dad had even drawn the mailbox they were hiding behind. "Is that me?" asked Max, pointing to a small stick man in a fedora.

Dad nodded.

"May I have the pencil?" asked Max.

Max drew glasses and a necktie on the stick Max. Then he drew a taller stick man next to it. The tall one had glasses on too, and a bandanna. Max would have drawn a mustache, but after Dad's mustache had fallen into his coffee, Dad had put it in his pocket instead of on his face.

"Nice details, Agent Pepperoni," said Dad. "Should we draw the man in the yellow shirt, too?"

The man in the yellow shirt! Max had almost forgotten about him! He looked up and down Birch Street. Finally, Max spotted him. The man had crossed the road and was about to enter another building. SHOPS ON BIRCH, it said above the door.

"We can't lose him!" said Max. He ran to the corner, and Dad followed, but just as they reached it, the streetlight turned red. Max hopped up and down. He wanted to keep running, but even spies needed to obey traffic signals.

At last the light turned green. Max and Dad ran across the intersection and down the street to Shops on Birch. Inside was a wide corridor lined with stores.

The man in the yellow shirt was gone.

"What next, Agent Pepperoni?" asked Dad.

Max was not sure. *The Sneaky Book of Spy Skills* had not covered this exact situation. Should they wait to see if the man in the yellow shirt came out of one of the shops? Or should they go look for him? What if the man came out of one shop while he and Dad were inside another? He might get away!

"You stay here and keep lookout," said Max, "and I will go in each shop and spy."

"Sorry, pal," said Dad. "I can't let you go running around in those stores by yourself." Dad did not sound like an army guy or a police officer or even Agent Cheese now. He sounded like a dad.

"I won't go running around," said Max. "Running is not inconspicuous. I will open each door and step inside—two steps. I will take three sneaky photos and then come right back out here where you can see me."

Dad thought for a minute. "Two steps?" he said.

"Two steps and three sneaky photos."

"And I'll stay right here and watch you?"

"You'll stay right here and watch for the man in the yellow shirt," said Max.

Dad nodded. "Okay, Agent Pepperoni. Get to work."

Max opened the door of the first shop and took two steps in. It was a toy store. There were games and puzzles and stuffed animals everywhere. A lumpy stuffed walrus stared at him from a nearby shelf. "Have you seen a dark-haired man in a yellow shirt?" Max asked the walrus.

"Excuse me?" said a skinny saleslady.

"Nothing," said Max. "Sorry." He took three sneaky photos—*snap snap snap*—and stepped out of the shop.

"Any luck, Agent Pepperoni?" asked Dad.

"Nope. How about you, Agent Cheese?"

"Nothing yet," said Dad.

Max dashed to the next shop. It was filled with cigars, and it smelled terrible. He held his breath, took his three sneaky photos—*snap snap snap*—and hurried back into the corridor.

"Anything?" he asked Dad.

"Nope," said Dad.

Max was beginning to get discouraged. He walked a little more slowly to the next store.

FRANZI'S CHOCOLATE FACTORY, it said on the door. Max took two steps inside. Franzi's Chocolate Factory did not smell like stinky cigars. It smelled like heaven.

"Be right with you," called a lady's voice.

A curtain at the back of the shop jiggled, and out from behind it walked a dark-haired man in a yellow T-shirt, but he was not the man Max had been following. Another man came out. He was wearing a yellow shirt too, but he was not the man Max had been following either. Another man followed and then another. And then several women and two children and a few more men, all in bright yellow T-shirts, all munching on large wedges of chocolate. And right behind them was a smiling lady in a pink apron.

"This is just a tour group," she said to Max. "You can

come in. I'll be right back." She disappeared behind the curtain again.

"Hello," said Max to the tour group.

"Hello," said the tour group to Max. The hello sounded very happy, but also a little different from the hellos Max was used to hearing.

"No English," said the man nearest him. "*Italiano?*"

"No *Italiano*," said Max.

The man shrugged and smiled and pointed at Max's hat. Then he pulled a camera from his

pocket. "Cheese?" he asked.

"Sure," said Max, smiling for a picture. *Snap* went the man's camera.

"Cheese?" asked Max, holding up his own camera. The man smiled. Max took three pictures that were not at all sneaky—*snap snap snap*—and hurried out of Franzi's Chocolate Factory.

"Agent Pepperoni!" said Dad. "You just missed him! The man in the yellow shirt went in there!" Dad pointed to a shop with wedding dresses in the window, just as the man in the yellow T-shirt came out.

Dad ducked behind a potted plant, but Max did not.

"Hello," said Max to the man.

"Hello," said the man to Max. His hello did not sound as happy as the tour group's had.

"Are you lost?" asked Max.

"No English," said the man in the yellow shirt.

Max held up his sneaky spy phone and showed the man in the yellow shirt the picture on the screen. "Ah!" said the man. Now he sounded happy.

"This way," said Max. He waved for the man in the yellow shirt to follow him. Then he waved for Dad. "Come on, Agent Cheese."

Dad and the man in the yellow shirt followed Max to Franzi's Chocolate Factory.

"Hello," said Max when he opened the door.

"AH!!" said the tour group.

"AH!" said the man in the yellow shirt.

"There you are!" said a lady with a yellow shirt and a yellow umbrella. She rushed up to the man, and they spoke in Italian. The man pointed to Max. "Cheese," he said.

"Pepperoni, actually," said Dad. "I'm Cheese."

"Well, thank you both," said the lady with the umbrella. "I was giving a tour of the neighborhood, and I didn't even notice that Mr. Benetti had wandered away. He couldn't call any of us because his phone battery died."

"Happy to help," said Max.

The lady in the pink apron gave Max and Dad each a large wedge of chocolate. They posed for a picture with Mr. Benetti. *Snap snap snap snap snap snap snap!* went all the cameras in the room.

"So much for being inconspicuous," said Dad. "I guess there'll be no spying in Italy for us. Our cover is blown."

Max took another bite of heavenly chocolate. "It's worth it."

Before he and Dad left Shops on Birch, Max needed to stop at the toy store.

"We found the man in the yellow shirt," he told the lumpy stuffed walrus when they walked into the shop. "I thought you'd want to know."

"Excuse me?" said the skinny saleslady.

"Nothing," said Max, pulling his spy hat down low.

Dad whispered something to the saleslady that Max did not hear.

"I'm sure we can arrange something," said the saleslady. "Hey, kiddo, come with me. Your dad thinks you might want to see the football trivia game we just got in."

"I'm going to use the restroom," said Dad. "Be right back."

Max followed the lady to the game section and half listened as she explained the football trivia game. Mostly, he took sneaky photos—*snap snap snap snap snap*—until she had run out of things to say and Dad came back.

"Did you gather any important information while I was away?" Dad asked Max, but the saleslady thought he was talking to her.

"I'm not sure your son cares that much about football," she said.

Dad looked surprised. The plastic scar Max had stuck on Dad's forehead wrinkled, then dropped to the floor.

Max handed it to Dad, who put it in his pocket with his mustache.

"We should leave, Agent Cheese," said Max. "Before our cover is blown here, too."

"Roger," said Dad. It was a pilot way to say "I agree," not a spy way, but on a day when a helper spy had already lost his scar and his mustache, it seemed nicer not to correct him.

"I told you I was a sneaky-photo expert," said Max.

As soon as they had returned to Dad's apartment, Dad had downloaded all the photos from Max's sneaky-spy camera onto his laptop so that they could look at them together. Some of the pictures were blurry, but the rest were interesting. The lady in the turban looked very nice, and so did the man in the yellow shirt. There were artistic-looking photos of people's legs and of the sky and the sidewalk. In the cigar store, Max had taken a

very funny photo of a man he had not even known was in the room. The man was adjusting his toupee.

There were photos of all the places on Dad's map, too. "A good day of important information gathering, Agent Cheese," said Max.

"I guess you got to see my new neighborhood after all," said Dad.

A loud *buzzzz* sounded from the box beside Dad's front door. Dad went to it, pushed a small button, and spoke into the box. "Hello?"

"Delivery," said a voice. "Pedro's Pizza and an extra package from—"

"Yes, yes. Okay," Dad interrupted. "Be right

back, Max." He left the apartment to meet the delivery man in the lobby, and Max went back to looking at his pictures.

So far, he liked the sneaky photos he had taken at the toy store the best. One made it look like a toy fire truck was flying through the air, and another showed the skinny saleslady's wrist tattoo. And . . . what was this one? A behind-the-back shot had caught an image of the cashier's stand and a man who looked a lot like Agent Cheese. The man had his wallet out, and something brown and stuffed and lumpy was sitting next to the cash register.

"Suspicious," said Max.

Max looked up as the apartment door opened and Dad backed into the kitchen. "Keep looking at your photos," called Dad. "I'll just get this pizza on some plates." From where he sat in the orange armchair, Max could see Dad's head and shoulders, but the breakfast bar blocked his view of the kitchen counter and the pizza.

"Very suspicious," said Max.

Dad set two plates of pizza on the breakfast bar. "Oh, shoot. I forgot the drinks in the fridge. Could you get them, Agent Pepperoni?"

Max set the laptop on the orange armchair and went into the kitchen to get the drinks. There on the counter was something lumpy and stuffed, wearing a hat and glasses. "What's this?" asked Max.

Dad leaned over the breakfast bar. "Hmm," he said. He reached to pull the hat and glasses off of the lumpy, stuffed thing. It was the walrus from the toy shop. "Oh! It's you, Agent Whiskers!" said Dad.

"Agent Whiskers?" asked Max.

"He's new to spying. He will need lots of training," said Dad.

"I can train him," said Max. "I trained you."

"Yes, you did," said Dad.

Max got the drinks, and Dad lifted Agent Whiskers up onto the breakfast bar. "He will need practice keeping secrets," said Dad.

"I can tell him mine," said Max. "When you're not around."

"As long as you fill me in on the weekends," said Dad. "I don't want to miss anything."

Max took a bite of pepperoni and nodded.

"I wonder if we should tell him a secret now, just for practice?" asked Dad. "Do you have any secrets right now?"

Max thought about it. He did have one secret. He whispered it in the spot where Agent Whiskers's ear would be if walruses had ears.

"Okay," said Dad. "Now tell me."

Max hesitated. "Tell you?"

"Otherwise, how will I know if Agent Whiskers spills the beans?" asked Dad.

Max got that someone-sitting-on-his-chest feeling again.

"It's okay," said Dad. "Main spies can tell their helper spies anything."

Max leaned over and put his mouth right next to Dad's ear, which was good, because then he would not have to see Dad's disappointed eyes. "I don't like football curtains," he whispered. "And I don't really like helmet lamps."

"That is important information," said Dad. "I'm glad you told me."

Max realized he had his eyes closed. He opened them and looked at Dad's face. If Dad had been

wearing his mustache, it would have fallen in his pizza. Dad was smiling. Max's someone-sitting-on-his-chest feeling vanished.

"Is there anything else you want to tell me, Agent Pepperoni?"

There was one more thing. "You're a good dad, Dad," said Max.

Dad hugged Max. "And you're a good son, son."

It was the most important information either of them had gathered all day.

WEEKEND
TWO

The
Blues

"You'll never defeat me, Baron Mincemeat! I'll never give—AAAAAAAAAHHHHHHHH!" Max flicked a plastic man off the plastic brick tower he had built. The man hit the hard wooden floor, and his head flew right off.

"Ha! Ha!" A second plastic man peered down from the tower at the headless body below. Max made his voice sound dark and evil. "Stevicus has fallen to his doom."

"Max?" said Dad. "Do you think your men could fall to their doom a little more quietly?"

Dad was sitting in the orange armchair. He had a ukulele in his lap. On the big TV was a movie, *Big Bad Blues*, that Dad had borrowed from Ace. Max had glanced at the movie a few times. It wasn't very interesting. The movies Max liked were action movies, which meant people were always chasing each other or jumping off cliffs or shooting bows and arrows. This movie was a documentary, which meant nobody did anything. They just sat there and talked.

The man on the TV had a guitar he said was named Bernadette. There had been times, he said, when Bernadette has been his only friend. Times when he was low-down and blue.

Blue was another word for *sad*, Max knew, but he liked picturing the guitar man holding his breath until he turned the same color as Max's bedroom walls. Dad had said he would repaint

those walls any color Max wanted, but once the football curtains and the helmet lamp had been swapped for regular red curtains and a regular red lamp, Max decided blue was fine. But it would be a pretty funny color for a guitar guy to be.

Baron Mincemeat turned his back on the broken Stevicus just as the man on the TV started a song. Max could hear Dad plucking the ukulele strings, trying to match the notes that the guitar man played. When the man sang, Dad said *Uh-huh* and *That's right*. The words in the song were about heartache and being broke and even the dog turning its back on you.

"He should sing about something else," said Max. "Then he wouldn't be so sad."

"Oh, yeah?" said Dad.

"He should sing about pizza or rockets or car chases," said Max. "He'd be happier."

"Maybe he would," said Dad. "But maybe it's the other way around. Maybe when you feel bad, you can sing things that you can't find words to say otherwise. Maybe songs help you sort through the sad or the bad or the uncomfortable."

Max knew about being uncomfortable. There were only three chairs in Dad's whole apartment, two tall stools at the breakfast bar and the orange armchair Dad was sitting in to watch his documentary. Max had been sitting on the hard wood floor all night. When he had been busy making adventures for Stevicus, this was okay. But now that Stevicus had met his doom, it was not.

"Ow-oooo. Ow-ooooo," sang Max. "I've got the sore-butt blues."

Dad laughed. "The what?"

Max made his face look sad, like the singer on *Big Bad Blues,* and sang:

"I'm sad because my butt hurts.
I've been sitting on the floor.
Yes, I'm sad because my butt hurts.
I've been sitting on the floor.
If I don't find a couch soon, baby,
I won't be coming here no more."

Dad laughed again, but his face looked a little bit like the guitar guy's had, too. He clicked off the TV. "It's late, son. Let's see if your bed is more comfortable."

"Just a minute," said Max. He popped Stevicus's head back on its body. If anything should give a person the blues, it would be having your head fly off, but Max did not think Stevicus would sing a song about it. Stevicus would wait for Max to snap him back together and then he would leap back into action.

"Sleep well, Baron Mincemeat," Max whispered in Stevicus's voice. "Tomorrow, we battle again."

"Ba-da ba-da ba-da ba-da BOP-doo-dow."

Dad had been humming the same tune all morning. At the coffee shop, Max heard him tell Ace that out of all the songs in *Big Bad Blues*, it was his favorite.

"I've been working on that one myself." Ace pulled his ukulele from under the counter and played a few notes. Everyone in the restaurant looked up expectantly. "I hope you're ordering the pancakes," Ace whispered to Max.

"Yep," said Max. Why wouldn't he order the pancakes? They were the County's Best. And Max liked the song that went with them. It was not a sad song. It was a funny song. The last rhyme in it was so bad that people always laughed, no matter how often they had heard it before.

"Are you going to Doctor Spin tonight?" Ace asked Dad.

Doctor Spin was the old-fashioned record store in town. "Why would we go to Doctor Spin?" asked Max.

"It's Open Mike Night," said Ace. "Anyone can perform."

"It's not a very kid-friendly event," said Dad.

Max pictured evil men like Baron Mincemeat scowling down at him. "I can take it," he said. "I'm tougher than you think."

"You're a brute," said Ace, sliding a cup of hot chocolate over to Max. "I can tell. But your dad's right. The language isn't always schoolyard appropriate. Some other time, Leo."

Dad had nodded and ordered his usual. Max peeked at him out of the corner of his eye. Dad had that guitar-man look on his face again. Did he have the blues because he couldn't go to Open Mike Night? Because he was stuck with Max? The thought made Max feel bad. Low-down and blue, even. Max did not like feeling low-down and blue.

He spun on the stool until his pancakes came. Then he ate them as fast as he could. And when he got outside, he ran and ran and ran.

Dad unlocked the apartment-building door. "I thought those pancakes would make you too slow to catch my mighty football passes," he said as Max sped into the lobby. "But I guess I was wrong."

"Race you up the stairs," said Max, but Dad pushed the elevator button.

Max hopped up and down while he waited for the elevator. He studied the mailboxes in the hallway. In the neighborhood where he lived with Mom, mailboxes sat on poles by the street. At

Dad's apartment, the mailboxes were built into the wall, and Dad needed a key to get his mail. Every mailbox had a label on it. B. COLLINS 104. T. TIBBET 302. Z. POLASKI 201. And Dad's: L. LeROY 202.

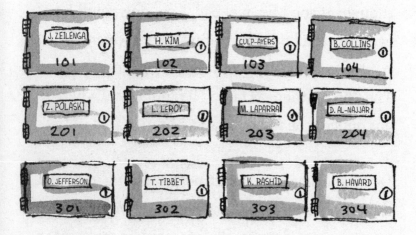

J. ZEILENGA 101
H. KIM 102
CULP-AYERS 103
B. COLLINS 104
Z. POLASKI 201
L. LEROY 202
M. LAPARRA 203
D. AL-NAJJAR 204
O. JEFFERSON 301
T. TIBBET 302
K. RASHID 303
B. HAVARD 304

Bing! The elevator door rumbled open. A small woman in a purple turban stepped out. She wore a puffy coat that reminded Max of a sleeping bag. The woman had on red rubber boots and thick red mittens, and in her hand she held the leashes of two sturdy basset hounds. Max remembered their names from when he and Dad had been spies and had overheard the woman talking to Ace. "Hi, Barkis!" he said. "Hello, Peggoty!"

The woman smiled, which made extra wrinkles on her already wrinkly face. One of the dogs flopped onto his back and scratched. The plumper one waddled closer, and Max held out his hand for the dog to sniff. The dog licked his sleeve.

"Syrup," said Dad.

"You must be 'L. LeRoy 202,'" said the woman.

"And son," said Dad.

Max dropped to his knees to pet the dog, who continued to sniff his clothes for traces of syrup. She found some on his coat collar and licked. Her breath smelled like vegetable soup.

"Theodosia Tibbet, 302," said the woman. The elevator rattled away to a higher floor. "Barkis, Peggoty, and I are in the apartment above you. You play some sort of stringed instrument."

"A ukulele," said Dad. "I'm just learning."

"Barkis likes it very much. He would howl along if I did not provide distraction."

Distraction sounded like a good idea to Max. The plumper dog was a determined syrup sniffer and had climbed onto his lap for better access. "What sort of distraction?" he asked as the dog licked his ear.

"Biscuits. Which then distract Peggoty, unless she is provided one as well. Since you have moved in, L. LeRoy, Peggoty has put on pounds. Thus," said the woman, jiggling the leashes, "we must brave the elephants." She winked at Max. "I mean elements, of course, but it seems more courageous to brave elephants than to fret about puddles, doesn't it?"

Max nodded. He liked Theodosia Tibbet. He could tell that she was the kind of person who would never sing the blues—no matter how sad or bad or uncomfortable things got. But he could also tell that she was in no hurry to go outside. It had rained last night and was damp and chilly out this morning. Max doubted that Ms. Tibbet would enjoy jumping over puddles.

"We were going upstairs to get our football to throw around at the park," said Max. "Maybe we could walk your dogs for you instead?"

Ms. Tibbet tilted her head as she thought. "Barkis and Peggoty are my heart and soul, but I am an indoor woman. I am also a good judge of character. I trust you," she said to Max. "And I know where to find your father, should I need to exact retribution."

"She means 'to get even with if something goes wrong,'" Dad said to Max.

"He knows what I mean," said Ms. Tibbet. Max had only sort of known what she meant, but he nodded. He liked having Ms. Tibbet think he was trustworthy and smart.

"Well?" said the woman to her dogs. As far as Max could tell, the dogs did not do anything different than they had been doing, but Ms. Tibbet had her answer. "Barkis is willing," she said. She chuckled as if she had made a joke, and Max chuckled too.

"A caution: These are not greyhounds. Their pace is not swift, and they like an intermission."

"Don't walk too fast and let them rest sometimes?" said Max.

"Exactly. Perhaps you could bring your instrument, L. LeRoy. I'm sure Barkis would enjoy an entertainment during his rest stops."

Max saw Dad's face light up.

"Now, that's an idea," said Dad. "Stay here, Max. I'll be right back."

Dad did not wait for the elevator to return to the lobby. He ran up the stairs.

CHAPTER

THREE

Peggoty was not fast like a greyhound. In fact, Max wondered if she was a hound at all. She was more like a nose with legs. All she wanted to do was sniff.

She sniffed at the sidewalk.

She sniffed at the trees.

She sniffed at a hat someone had dropped on the ground.

She sniffed at garbage cans and fire hydrants and mailboxes.

She sniffed as she walked through puddles, dragging her ears like flat-bottomed boats.

"C'mon, Peggoty," said Max each time she stopped to sniff.

He supposed he should be happy the dog was such a slowpoke. Just before they left the apartment building, Dad had told Ms. Tibbet that they would not be long because he and Max had some shopping to do that afternoon.

Max hated shopping. It was boring. Back when his parents still lived together, one of them usually stayed home with Max while the other went shopping, but now it felt like Max had to go on every errand to every store in the state. "Oh, Max," his mom had said once, "it's not *that* boring. At least you get to walk around and look at things. It's not like you're penned up in a jail cell. *That* would be boring."

Mom had been wrong. Max would rather be in jail than go shopping. In jail you could sneak a spoon out of the cafeteria and dig a tunnel and escape. There was no escape from the grocery store.

Peggoty stopped to sniff again. This time, Max could not blame her. They were just outside Lickety Split Ice Cream. Max took a big sniff too. It smelled like chocolate and caramel and vanilla and nuts.

"Keep her moving, Max," said Dad. "Or we'll

never make it to the park." Barkis trotted ahead with Dad.

"C'mon, Peggoty," said Max. The basset hound looked up at him. Okay, so she wasn't just a nose with legs. She also had sad, sad eyes.

"*Wumph,*" she said.

"I know," said Max.

Oak Grove Park took up a whole block. It did not have a playground, like the park near Max's house with Mom. It had a fountain and trees and a long, curvy path. Dad chose a bench with a view of the entire park. He pulled a bandanna from his pocket, dried off the bench seat, and sat down. Barkis and Peggoty flopped in front of him and panted. Everyone was ready for an intermission. Except Max.

"Can I run on the path?" he asked.

Dad lifted his ukulele from its case and looked around the park. "I guess so. I can keep our canine companions entertained."

Before Dad could play a single note, Max was running. He jumped over  puddles. He jumped over spots where he wished puddles had been. It had been hard to walk as slow as Peggoty. It had been hard to stop for every sniff. Now Max ran like a rocket, around a tree and past the fountain. He could not hear Dad's ukulele when he ran, but he could hear Barkis howl.

"Stevicus was only a few yards ahead of the Baron's men," said Max. He imagined himself running through a dark green forest. On his back, he had tied a sack that held the Orb of All Time. If he let it fall into the Baron's hands, the Baron would stop time for everyone but himself and his men. They would steal all the jewels and money and stuff, and the rest of the people could do nothing about it. They would be frozen in time and totally bored forever.

Zing! The Baron's men were shooting arrows! "Stevicus dodged them, darting left and right. He leaped high into the air, but landed on a  slippery rock and fell, just as another arrow whizzed overhead."

Max landed on the damp grass, somersaulted, and sprang to his feet. "Stevicus patted himself on the back—but not because he was conceited or anything. He was checking for the Orb of All Time. It was still there. The world was safe."

Max ran the entire path twice, then dropped onto the bench beside Dad. His heart thumped a happy, run-around-the-park thump. Peggoty

sniffed his knees where he had fallen in the grass. Her tail thunked on the dirt, in time with Max's heartbeat.

"I think Peggoty likes you," said Dad.

"I think Barkis liked your music," said Max. "I heard him howling."

Dad scratched Barkis's ear. "Nothing in the world like an appreciative audience," he said.

If Dad could go to Open Mike Night, he would have an audience, Max thought. His heart continued to thump, but it didn't feel as happy as it had before.

"I'm going to run one more lap," said Max.

"Can't, pal," said Dad. "I promised Ms. Tibbet we wouldn't have Barkis and Peggoty out for too long." Dad stood and slung his ukulele case over his shoulder. "Besides, we have some shopping to do."

Max took Peggoty's leash and followed Dad, but he was imagining Stevicus kneeling behind a tree. *Stevicus took the Orb of All Time from its sack and gasped,* Max said in his head. *He had saved the Orb from the Baron's men, but it had cracked. Stevicus could feel the freezy boredom leaking out. It felt just like shopping.*

The INEEDA furniture store sold everything from pencil holders to kitchen sinks. Every item in the store had a name, which made Max laugh. "This is my toothbrush Albert," he said to Dad. Except the toothbrush he had picked up off the display had not been named Albert. It had been named "Tandborste," which made Max laugh even harder.

Dad did not laugh. "We don't need tooth-brushes today," he said. "We need to cure your sore-butt blues. We need a sofa."

The furniture store was so big that the salespeople had given them a map when they came in. Dad used it to get them to the SOFA/COUCH section pretty quickly. This gave Max hope that their shopping would be fast and they would go home soon. But when they reached the sofas, everything changed.

Dad was the slowest sofa shopper in history.

He considered every sofa in the store.

He stood in front of them.

He leaned against them.

He sat on one end and slid to the other.

He kicked off his shoes and stretched across them.

And then, when Max thought he must have made up his mind that this was the best sofa in the place, Dad would get up and stand in front of another one. The whole time, he hummed the *ba-da, ba-da* blues song.

Max wondered if this was taking so long because Dad was really thinking about Open Mike Night. Sometimes it was hard for Max to focus on his homework sheets when he was thinking about playing basketball with his friend Warren or building a fort for Stevicus. Maybe Dad was wishing he could go to Open Mike Night as much as Max was wishing he could leave this furniture store.

Dad stood in front of another sofa. "What do you think of this one?" he asked Max.

Max read the tag that hung from the sofa's arm. "Its name is Flenn, which reminds me of this kid in my class named Glenn. I don't think I could watch TV while sitting on Glenn."

"I'm serious, Max," said Dad.

Max looked at Flenn. It looked like a couch. "It's fine," he said.

"Surely you have more to say than that," said Dad.

Max had lots of things to say, but he did not have the words to say them. He remembered what Dad had said about the blues—how people found words to sing what they couldn't say. Did that really work? Max looked at Flenn again. It had ugly black horizontal stripes. He heard the *ba-da, ba-da* blues song in his head.

"*The stripes look like a jail suit. Gives me the prison-couch blues,*" sang Max. He sang it quietly, but Dad heard.

"The prison-couch blues?"

Max shrugged.

"I guess it does look a little penitential," said Dad. "What about this one?"

Dad had Max sit on a red couch named Ploomf.

"*It's sticky and it smells like plastic,*" sang Max. "*I got the sticky-red-plastic blues.*"

"Okay. No jail stripes. No sticky. No plastic." Dad moved to a couch that was soft and brown and nubby. "How about this one? It reminds me of Agent Whiskers."

Probably that was a good thing, but Max did not want it to be. He did not feel like saying anything was good. He felt like getting out of here.

"What's good about a walrus isn't always good about a sofa." Max flopped onto a gray couch named Olle and crossed his arms.

Dad sat down beside him. "I wish you'd help me out," he said. "I don't want to goof up and get the wrong thing, like I did with the football curtains."

"What you really wish is that you didn't have me tonight, so you could go to Open Mike Night at Doctor Spin," said Max. There. He had said it. And he didn't need some old blues song to do it.

"Oh, Max." Dad leaned back on Olle and looked at the ceiling. Max did the same. "Open Mike Night at Doctor Spin is not for kids, but this has nothing to do with you. The truth is I'm not a good enough player."

Max sat up. "Yes, you are, Dad. You're great!"

Dad fiddled with a green plastic squirrel named Knut that had been perched on the end table beside him.

"I don't like making mistakes, especially big mistakes that everyone can see. Or hear."

Max understood this. He was better at dribbling a basketball in the driveway at Mom's than he was at school with his whole class watching. But Mr. Sherwin, his P.E. teacher, said the only way to get better was to practice with other kids around, and eventually he would forget people were looking.

Max told Dad what Mr. Sherwin had said.

"Has it worked?" asked Dad.

"I'm a lot better at dribbling. I'm a little better about forgetting that people are looking."

"Hmm," said Dad. It was the *hmm* sound Dad made when he was really thinking about something. He stretched his arm along the top of the couch, and Max leaned back like he had before. They sat there for a while, and Max closed his eyes. It felt good. It wasn't even boring.

"You two moving in?" A salesman in a bright blue shirt was standing over them.

"My dad already has an apartment," said Max.

"But I don't have a sofa," said Dad, patting the arm of the couch. It made a solid thunking sound. "Max, what do you think of Olle?"

Max considered Olle.

He stood in front of it.

He leaned against it.

He sat on one end and slid to the other.

He kicked off his shoes and stretched across it.

Then he got back up and stood in front of Olle again.

"Well?" said the salesman.

"Just a minute," said Max. He peered beneath the sofa. There was just enough room to crawl under.

Stevicus snuck into the tiny crevice and watched as the Baron's men stomped stupidly past, said Max in his head. *While he waited, he checked the Orb of All Time. The crack was gone. It was a miracle!*

Max shimmied out from his hiding place and crouched behind the sofa. *What Stevicus needed now was a hideout. But where could he go? An arrow zipped overhead. He had been spotted! "We will exact retribution!" shouted one of the Baron's men. Stevicus dove for cover. He landed on something soft and bouncy and safe. It was the perfect hideout.*

"Well?" said the salesman again.

Max looked at Dad and nodded.

"We'll take it," they said together.

It turned out that they could not bring Olle home with them that afternoon. The salesman said that the sofa would be delivered later in the week and until then, if they had guests, it would have to be B.Y.O.C.

"What's B.Y.O.C.?" Max asked Dad as they waited at the cash register. In addition to paying for Olle, Dad was buying the green plastic Knut and a bag of dog biscuits named Voff-Voff that Max had picked up for Barkis and Peggoty.

"Bring Your Own Chair, I guess," said Dad. "The sales guy was being funny. Sometimes parties are B.Y.O.B., which means Bring Your Own Beverage."

Dad paid the cashier and tucked Knut under his arm. He handed the dog treats to Max.

"If you were having a dog party, it could mean Bring Your Own Biscuits," said Max as they headed to the car.

"I suppose it could," said Dad.

"If you were a lion, it could be B.Y.O.Z."

"Bring Your Own . . . Zebra?" Dad laughed. "Max, that's gruesome!"

Max leaped over a parking-lot puddle. He loved making Dad laugh.

"Do you know any funny ukulele songs?" Max asked as he got into the car.

"I know 'Yes, We Have No Bananas,'" said Dad. "Why?"

"I think you should go to Open

Mike Night tonight and play a funny song. I can go with you. I will close my ears if anyone says any bad words."

Dad laughed again, even though Max had not meant to be funny. "I'm not going to Open Mike Night tonight—but who knows? I may surprise us both and go to the next one, whether I think I'm ready or not." Dad fastened his seat belt. "I just hope the audience is friendly to beginners."

Max hoped so too. He buckled his own seat belt and hoped that when Dad finally went to Open Mike Night, the audience would love his playing as much as Barkis did.

And that gave Max an idea.

If he were in his bedroom at his house with Mom, Max would have used colorful markers and construction paper for the invitation, but he did not think Dad had any art stuff in his apartment. Max did not ask, because then Dad might get suspicious. Max wanted everything to be a surprise.

Max wrote in boxy capital letters on the white page. He filled in the letters with dots and checks and stripes, so that even though the invitation was only in pencil, it would still look nice.

He folded the invitation into an origami football, tucked it in his pocket, and walked out to the kitchen. "I'm going upstairs to bring Barkis and Peggoty a Voff-Voff," he said to Dad.

"Okay," said Dad. "But don't stay long. Our pizza will be here any minute."

Max did not stay long. He gave a treat to each

of the dogs, handed Ms. Tibbet the folded-up invitation, and ran back down the stairs. He was so excited, he jumped the last three steps.

"You beat the pizza guy," said Dad when Max returned. Max checked the microwave clock: 6:50. In ten minutes, Ms. Tibbet would arrive.

Max had to move quickly. His Stevicus stuff was all over the floor. He scooped up the pieces and tossed them into their plastic bin. He shoved the bin behind the orange chair and looked around.

The room looked neat, but it also looked empty. When Ms. Tibbet and the dogs arrived, it would be better, but Max still wished Dad's Open

Mike Night audience could be bigger. He spotted Knut on the breakfast bar and sat him on the floor next to the orange armchair.

Better.

He got Agent Whiskers from the blue bedroom and sat him next to Knut.

Even better. But still kind of empty.

Max opened the plastic bin and took out Stevicus and Baron Mincemeat and all of the Baron's men. He sat them in front of Knut. "Don't make any false moves," Max made Stevicus say to the other plastic men. "Or my enormous trained

squirrel will attack." The Baron's men quivered with fear, but they did not try to escape.

Just then, there was a knock on the door.

"I wonder how the pizza guy got in the building without buzzing?" said Dad as he stepped out of the kitchen. "Max, would you get my wallet out of my room?"

Max ran to Dad's room. He was so excited that his stomach felt like a popcorn popper. He bounced across Dad's bed, found the wallet on the cardboard box Dad was using as a bedside table, and hopped back to the living room. The living room did not look empty any longer. Now it looked very full.

Ms. Tibbet had arrived with Barkis and Peggoty. Standing behind her were two other people that Max had never seen before: a plump man with a big nose and a gray mustache and a plump girl with a not-so-big nose and a one-armed baby doll. The man had three lawn chairs folded under

his arm. Beside him on the floor sat a shiny red suitcase.

"It was not the pizza guy at the door," said Dad. He gave Max a do-you-know-what's-going-on-here look.

"I have brought along Mr. Polaski," said Ms. Tibbet. "He has brought along his accordion and his niece, Estelle."

"I have a kazoo," said Estelle. She looked like

she was three or four years old. "And Monica." She held the one-armed baby doll out for Max to see.

"Z. Polaski, 201." Mr. Polaski held out his free hand to shake Dad's. "Where should I put these?"

"I—I don't know. I—" stammered Dad.

Dad gave Max another confused look. Max thought the popcorn popper in his stomach might explode. "You said you might surprise yourself and do Open Mike Night someday," said Max. "So . . . SURPRISE! Today is someday!"

"It certainly is," said Dad.

The pizza arrived as Mr. Polaski was unfolding the chairs. Dad had only four plates, so Max ate his pizza out of a bowl. When the pizza was gone, Max clapped his hands for attention.

"Welcome to Open Mike Night," he said. "Everyone gets to play, and nobody has to worry about mistakes. Who wants to go first?"

"Uncle Zeb goes first," said Estelle.

Mr. Polaski played a song he said was called "Lady of Spain." The fingers on his right hand hopped along the accordion keys; the fingers of his left hand danced on glossy black buttons. He pulled and squeezed the accordion open and shut, open and shut. Mr. Polaski closed his eyes while he played. As far as Max could tell, he did not make a single mistake.

"Bravo!" said Ms. Tibbet when he had finished. Barkis and Peggoty had fallen asleep at her feet, but when she spoke, their tails thumped on the wood floor.

"I go first next," said Estelle.

Estelle played her kazoo. Max could not tell if she made any mistakes, because he could not tell if she was even playing a song.

"Brava!" said Ms. Tibbet when Estelle had finished. The dog tails thumped again, and Ms. Tibbet stood.

"I do not possess the gift of music," she said. "Unless one counts poetry as song—which I do." Ms. Tibbet recited a poem she said was from Shakespeare. The dog tails thumped like drums.

Mr. Polaski whispered in Max's ear. "Theodosia used to be a teacher."

When Ms. Tibbet's poem was over, Max did not know whether to say *Bravo* or *Brava,* so he just clapped.

"And now you, L. LeRoy," said Ms. Tibbet.

Dad brought out his ukulele and tuned it. "I'm just a beginner," he said nervously.

"Tut, tut," said Ms. Tibbet. "You heard our Master of Ceremonies. We are not to worry about mistakes."

"Right," said Dad. He cleared his throat. "Um. This one is for Max." He strummed a tune Max had never heard before. It was peppy and sounded like smiling. Then Dad started singing about having no bananas. The words came very fast and Dad stumbled over a few of them, but Mr. Polaski and Ms. Tibbet joined in anyway.

Max wished he knew the words so he could sing too. Not knowing the words did not stop Estelle. "*Bananas, bananas, bananas,*" she sang.

Barkis howled.

Max ran to the kitchen to get some Voff-Voffs just as Dad finished his song. Everyone laughed and cheered.

"Bravissimo!" said Ms. Tibbet. Max gave Barkis and Peggoty each a treat.

"Thank you," said Ms. Tibbet. "And what will you be performing this evening, Max?"

Max had not thought that he would have to perform. He did not want to. He looked at Dad.

"Max is more of a songwriter than a performer," said Dad. "Am I right, Max?"

Max nodded.

"Well then, perhaps you will compose something for our next Open Mike Night," said Ms. Tibbet.

Max looked at Dad again. Dad's fingers were plucking softly at the ukulele strings, as if he were deciding what song he would play the next time.

"Okay," Max told Ms. Tibbet. "I will."

Max was not sure what the words would say, but he knew his song would be about what he was feeling right now. He already had a title. He would call his song "The Too Happy to Have Anything Sad to Sing About Blues."

Habitat

CHAPTER

ONE

The clock in Mrs. Maloof's classroom was broken. It had to be. It felt to Max like hours had passed since he last looked at it, but the skinny minute hand had moved only two notches.

When would school end?

Max's leg bounced under his desk. His best friend Warren's leg bounced too. Today, at 3:15, Dad would pick them both up from school and take them to his apartment. Warren was coming for a sleepover.

The last time he and Warren had a sleepover was in the summer, on the weekend Dad had moved out of Max's house and into the guest room at Grandma's. Max had gone to Warren's house,  and Warren's mom, Mrs. Sistrunk, had taken them to the movies and for ice cream and swimming at Stony Creek. That day, Max had been too busy to think about what was going on at his house. And that night, when Max did think about it, Warren had let him borrow his stuffed monkey, Bulldozer, to sleep with, which had been a good best-friend thing to do.

Now it was Max's turn to have Warren over. Warren did not have anything he had to be too busy to think about, but

Max had the whole sleepover planned out anyway.

After school, they would play Stevicus and then they would walk Barkis and Peggoty to the park, where he and Warren would run on the path and pretend that the joggers were Baron Mincemeat's men. When they got home, Dad would order pizza and they would watch an action movie on the big TV. On Saturday morning, they would go to Ace's and order the County's Best Bacon and Pineapple Pancakes so Warren could hear the pancake song. And when that was done, they would go back to Dad's apartment and finish their mammal projects before Warren's mom came to pick him up in the afternoon.

Max's leg bounced even faster.

"Don't forget. Your Michigan mammal reports and habitat models are due Monday," said Mrs. Maloof. "You need to finish everything over the weekend. Got it, friends?"

"Got it," said the class, but some of them sounded worried.

Max wasn't worried. The hard part was done. He had his report on the porcupine all written and illustrated and stapled together. The cover was especially good. He had drawn a picture of a porcupine eating a branch. He had drawn each quill individually, instead of scribbling up and down on the porcupine's back. It had taken a very long time.

His whole report had taken a long time. There was a lot to learn about porcupines. Everybody knew porcupines had cool quills, but Max had learned that porcupines were the second largest of all Michigan rodents. (Beavers were first. Warren had chosen beavers.) He also knew that porcupine babies were called porcupettes, which was a way better name than kits or pups or cubs. Lots of other mammal babies were called kits or pups or cubs. No other baby was called a porcupette.

Best of all, porcupine habitat was interesting. Porcupines lived mostly in the woods. They slept in dens in the super-cold winter, but when it was nice out, they liked to sleep in the crook of a tree branch. They could sleep for hours up there without falling off, just as cozy as if it were a bunk bed.

"Please go put your reports in your backpacks," said Mrs. Maloof. "When you return, we'll have Read Aloud."

Max slipped his report into the clear plastic envelope Mrs. Maloof had given them to protect their work and carried it out to the hall. When he got to his backpack, he tried to slide his report inside, but it was too tight a fit. To make room, he took out the plastic bag of habitat-making supplies he had brought from home and set it on the bench. In the plastic bag was a shoebox and paints and glue and a clay porcupine that Mom had helped him make. Mom had also helped him gather a bunch of odds and ends for making a forest floor.

Max tucked his report gently into his backpack. Before he zipped it closed, he could not help but look at the porcupine cover one more time.

* * *

Read Aloud made the rest of the day speed by. When Mrs. Maloof set down her copy of *The BFG* and said it was time to go home, Max was almost disappointed.

Almost, but not really.

"Let's go, let's go!" said Warren. He and Max quick-walked to the hallway. Dad was already there, holding Max's coat and backpack in his arms.

"Do you boys have everything?" asked Dad. His voice sounded funny. Slow and stuffy.

"Yep," said Max, grabbing his weekend bag off his coat hook.

"Yep!" said Warren, swinging his sleepover bag over his shoulder.

"I hope your cold gets better, Mr. LeRoy," said Mrs. Maloof.

Dad sniffed. "I don't have a cold," he said. It sounded more like *I dode hab a code.* "I never get colds."

Mrs. Maloof lifted an eyebrow the way she did when one of her students forgot a math packet at home. "Well then, have a good weekend!"

"We will!" said Max and Warren at the very same time. They quick-walked down the hall so fast it looked like they were running, but they weren't.

Dad trailed behind them.

Dad opened the apartment-building door, and Max and Warren quick-walked inside. "This is the lobby, and this where the mailboxes are." Max tapped mailbox 202. "This is Dad's. L. LeRoy."

"What is the *L* for?" asked Warren.

"Today? Lethargy," said Dad. Max could tell Dad was being funny, but he did not get the joke. "*Lethargy* means having very little energy. Being slow-moving. I guess I didn't sleep well last night." Dad sniffed and pushed the elevator button.

"Warren and I have lots of energy," said Max. "We'll take the stairs."

Dad nodded. Max and Warren quick-walked through the lobby and up the stairs. On the second floor, Max continued the tour. "This is the laundry room, and this is 201, where Mr. Polaski lives—he plays the accordion—and this is my dad's apartment."

"You always call it your dad's apartment," said Warren. "But it's your apartment too, isn't it?"

Max guessed it was, but it felt weird to say. His house had always been the one that he lived in with Mom. When he said "home," that was the place he thought of, not this new place he visited on the weekends. Max was glad to hear the elevator doors open before he had to explain any of that to Warren.

"Back up, boys," said Dad. "Make way for the man with the keys—*achoooo!*"

"Are you sure you don't have a cold, Mr. LeRoy?" asked Warren.

"I don't get colds," said Dad. "It must be allergies."

Dad opened the door, and they all went inside.

"This is the front hall. It isn't really a room. It's just a place to stand," said Max. "And this is the kitchen."

"It is very clean," said Warren. "Our kitchen is never this clean."

"That's because your parents actually use it to cook things," said Dad. "Why don't you boys put your stuff in Max's room?"

Max and Warren brought their bags and coats to the room with the blue walls. Warren unrolled his sleeping bag next to Max's bed and sat Bulldozer on it. Max pulled Agent Whiskers from his weekend bag and set him on the silver bedspread.

"Do you want to see the rest"—Max almost said *of my dad's apartment*—"of the place?"

"Okay," said Warren.

Max showed Warren the bathroom and Dad's white bedroom with the cardboard boxes and the living room with the orange armchair and the big TV and the new gray sofa.

"Our sofa's name is Olle. I picked him out," said Max.

"Your couch has a name?" said Warren.

"Dad wanted one named Flenn, but it rhymed with—"

"Glenn!" said Warren. "No way would I want to sit on Glenn!"

"That's what I said!" said Max. This was one more reason he and Warren were such good friends. They said the same things and ate the same things and liked to do the same things too.

"Did you bring your Stevicus?" asked Max.

"He's in my bag," said Warren.

Warren's Stevicus had tooth marks from Warren's dog, Laverne, but otherwise the two plastic men were exactly the same. Max and

Warren usually pretended the two heroes were twins, one named Steve and the other named Cuss. Baron Mincemeat's men were no match for the brothers.

"Look out, Cuss!" hollered Steve. Steve had reached the top of the silver cliff, but Cuss was still climbing the slippery rockface. Baron Mincemeat's men were down below, aiming their deadly arrows right at him.

"Got . . . to keep . . . go . . . ing," Warren made Cuss say as he climbed. "If I can just . . . make it . . ." Suddenly, Cuss was startled by a terrible roaring sound.

"What was that?" asked Warren.

Max had been so focused on the adventure that he had not noticed anything. "There are lots of extra noises in apartments," he said. "It's just other people or the heater or something."

"What kind of something?" asked Warren.

Max listened. This time he heard it, loud and clear.

"Sounds like a terrible monster has entered the forest," said Steve.

"Let's investigate," said Cuss.

The Baron's men howled with rage as Max and Warren took the heroes off to the living room.

"*SNNNNOOOORRRRGGGGGGHH!*" Dad was slouched on Olle, hands at his sides, head tilted back, asleep.

"Wow," said Warren.

Dad jumped. "Huh? What? You okay, Max?" he said, except *Max* sounded more like *Bax*. "What time is it? I'd better order the pizza."

"But we were going to walk Barkis and Peggoty first, remember?"

"I'm sorry, pal. I guess I fell asleep. It is a little late for that and, we—we—*wah—wwaaaaaah-choo!*" Dad dashed to the bathroom for a tissue and came back wiping his nose. "We'll walk the dogs tomorrow, okay? How about I order pizza and you guys pick out your movie?"

The movie was one of Max's favorites. It had so much running and climbing and jumping that Max found it difficult to sit on Olle to watch. Several times, he and Warren leaped from their seats so Steve and Cuss could reenact a scene. Despite all the action, Dad kept falling asleep. Max had to wake him so his snores wouldn't drown out the movie hero's battle cries.

When the movie was over, Max and Warren ran to the blue room and jumped onto the bed. "Settle down, boys," called Dad. "You need your rest."

Max knew that it was Dad who felt like resting, but that was okay. He emptied his weekend bag onto the floor. Warren did the same with his sleepover stuff, which landed with a thump.

"That's the logs for my beaver habitat," said Warren. "My lodge is done, but I need to finish the dam." He picked up the shoebox that had tumbled from his bag. There was a forest scene painted on

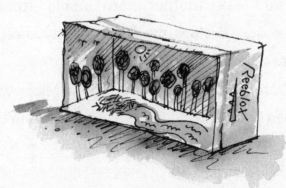

the back wall and a blue construction-paper pond on the bottom. Warren had glued a bunch of sticks together to make the beaver lodge. It was a lot further along than Max's habitat project.

"All I have so far is my supplies," said Max. "But I already made a clay porcupine."

He looked around for the plastic bag he and Mom had packed. It was not with his weekend things. He opened his school backpack. His porcupine report was there, but his supplies were not. Then he remembered. He had taken the bag out of his backpack to make room for his report.

"Oh, no!" said Max. "I left it at school!"

"Maybe we can go get it," said Warren.

"The school is probably locked for the weekend," said Max. Another snore rumbled from the living room. "Besides, my dad is already asleep. I'll have to tell him tomorrow."

Warren got into his sleeping bag. Max crawled into bed and turned out the light. For a long time,

Steve and Cuss talked in the dark. Eventually, Warren fell asleep.

Later—after crafting a detailed plan for how he and Warren and Dad could use sneaky spy tricks to slip into the school and rescue his porcupine supplies—Max fell asleep too.

The sneaky-spy porcupine-rescue plan did not seem as practical by day as it had when Max was falling asleep, but by the time he and Dad and Warren had arrived at Ace's Coffee Shop, Max was no longer thinking about porcupines anyway. Max was thinking about breakfast.

"I'll have the County's Best Bacon and Pineapple Pancakes," said Max. He was so excited that Warren was here at his favorite restaurant that he spun on his stool.

"Ditto," said Warren, who spun as well.

"Two orders of the County's Best, coming up!" Ace reached under the counter and pulled out his red ukulele. He plucked a string. Everyone in the coffee shop fell silent. Ace sang:

"Pancakes, oh pancakes,
oh pancakes divine.
Better with bacon,
much better with pine . . . apple.
Best in the county,
best we can make 'em.

Best with pineapple,
and bester with bac-om!"

The room burst into applause, but Ace held up a hand for quiet. "For a second order, a second verse!"

A second verse? Max had not known there was a second verse! This day was turning out great!

"Pancakes, oh pancakes,
oh pancakes galore.
Butter to slather,
syrup that's pour . . . able.
Some folks like whipped cream,
some prefer jelly.
Isn't much difference
when they're in your belly!"

What if there was a third verse? "Dad," cried Max, "order the pancakes! We need to see if there's a third verse!"

"I'm sorry, boys. I don't think I can handle the County's Best today." Dad knocked over a toothpick dispenser as he reached for a napkin. "It feels like a coffee-and-dry-toast day to me," he said, wiping his nose.

Ace set the toothpick dispenser back on its feet. "You'll have to come back on a day when your dad doesn't have a cold."

"Mr. LeRoy doesn't get colds," said Warren.

"Good to know," said Ace, but Max saw him raise his eyebrow, just like Mrs. Maloof had.

After breakfast, Max and Warren ran all the way to Dad's apartment, though they had to double back for Dad several times.

"Let's take a

breather before we walk the dogs," said Dad when they finally reached 202. Max and Warren quick-walked to the room with the blue walls to get Steve and Cuss.

Warren's habitat project was on the dresser. As soon as Max saw it, he remembered. His great-day feeling vanished. How was he going to make a porcupine habitat without any supplies?

"Does your dad have markers?" asked Warren. "For work, maybe?"

A huge snore echoed in the living room. Dad was asleep again. "My dad is a systems analyst," said Max. "I don't think they use markers."

"Too bad he's not an artist," said Warren. "Or a teacher. A teacher would have markers and paints and stuff."

A teacher! Didn't Mr. Polaski say that Ms. Tibbet used to be a teacher? The day was saved!

Max left Dad a note.

Visiting Ms. Tibbet, 302

Max and Warren tiptoed out of the apartment. They shut the door behind them very quietly.

"Are you being sneaky?" said a loud voice.

It was Mr. Polaski's plump niece, Estelle. She had yellow stuff all over her face and hands. It looked like she had been attacked by a mustard sandwich.

"We're doing important homework," whispered Max.

"Can I do it too?" Estelle asked just as loudly as before.

"Sorry," said Max. "This is third-grader stuff. Besides, shouldn't you be with your uncle?"

"He said stand right here until he could get a washcloth."

"You'd better do what he says, then," said Max. He grabbed Warren's arm. They quick-walked to the stairs as fast as they could.

"I have a black marker I use to address packages," said Ms. Tibbet. "But I am afraid I have no paints." She invited Max and Warren into 302. Its walls were not white but bright purple, most of which was hidden behind tall bookshelves. "Sit," she said. Max and Warren sat. So did Barkis and Peggoty.

"Tell me why you need paints," she said.

Max and Warren explained everything, including how they thought she might have art supplies, since she used to be a teacher.

"I was once a professor of English literature. Although I enjoyed it very much, it was sadly lacking in painting opportunities," said Ms. Tibbet.

"However, I have read a few things that may help. Are you boys familiar with the term *quest*?"

Stevicus went on quests all the time. "It's like a mission to find something and there are battles and stuff along the way," said Max.

"Precisely—although I hope today's journey will prove battle-free," said Ms. Tibbet. "I propose a quest. Two young heroes—"

"That means us," Max said to Warren.

"Two companionable beasts—" Ms. Tibbet continued.

"That means the dogs."

"And one elderly sage."

Max didn't want to call Ms. Tibbet elderly, so he didn't say anything, but Warren understood.

"A smart lady," said Warren.

Ms. Tibbet smiled her wrinkle-making smile and handed Max a pencil and paper. "Make a list of quest items. I will call L. LeRoy and inform him of our plans."

The list looked like this:

Forest floor stuff
Box
Paint
Glue
Trees
Rocks

Max showed Warren the list. "I have Super Sticky Glue in my bag," said Warren.

Max crossed glue off the list.

"One quest item already in hand?" said Ms. Tibbet. "That bodes well. Now, shall we commence?"

"Yes," said Max. "Let's go."

It was a beautiful, sunny day. Max was so excited to be going on a quest that he wanted to run, but when they got outside, Ms. Tibbet handed him Peggoty's leash. She gave Barkis's leash to Warren.

"I find it easier to be a sage when I am not being dragged about by beasts." Ms. Tibbet looked at the list of quest items. "'Forest floor stuff,'" she read.

"Leaves and pebbles," explained Max. "Maybe some small sticks."

"And where in all the land might such treasures be discovered?" asked Ms. Tibbet.

Max thought. "The park?" he said.

"Indeed," said Ms. Tibbet. "The park shall be our destination. But perhaps we should consider other stops along the way?"

"Toothpicks could be sticks," said Max. "Ace's Coffee Shop has toothpicks."

"Onward, then, to Ace's," said Ms. Tibbet in a noble voice.

The young heroes led the companionable beasts and the elderly sage to the sidewalk in front of Ace's Coffee Shop. "I shall mind the hounds while you venture in," said Ms. Tibbet.

"Aren't you coming with us?" Max liked Ace, but he had never been inside the coffee shop without Dad. Going inside and finding Ace and asking for a favor made Max feel nervous.

Ms. Tibbet shook her head. "The role of the elderly sage is one of advisor. It is the young heroes' job to obtain the treasures of the quest."

"Shoot," said Warren. "I think she's right."

Max and Warren handed the leashes to Ms. Tibbet and pushed open the coffee-shop door. It looked different without Dad there. Darker and stuffier and like there were more strangers inside. When Max was little and had felt nervous, he always reached for Mom's or Dad's hand, but he was nine now, and there was no way he was holding hands with Warren.

They walked shoulder to shoulder up to the counter, where Ace was taking an order. Max had never noticed the scar on Ace's forearm before, or how huge his hands were. Ace gripped his order pencil like he might snap it in half. Max couldn't say a word. Even when Warren elbowed him, Max did not speak. Finally, Ace looked their way.

"Max, where's your dad?"

All the people at the counter turned to stare at Max. He felt like he could hear them

thinking, *A little boy? All alone?* He imagined them rubbing their hands together like Baron Mincemeat's men did when they were plotting something terrible.

"He—he's at home, sleeping," Max said. "We have Ms. Tibbet."

"She's an elderly sage," explained Warren.

"True," said Ace. "So, what can I do for you?"

Max cleared his throat. He tried to sound like a young hero. "We come in quest of toothpicks," he said.

"For a porcupine habitat," said Warren.

"For school," said Max.

The people at the counter laughed. At first it sounded like an evil Baron Mincemeat kind of laugh, but when Max looked at their faces, he could see it was the happy kind.

"I can help with that," said Ace. "Just a minute."

Ace disappeared into the kitchen. He came back a few minutes later with two bags. He handed one to Warren. "Toothpicks for school," he said. He handed the other bag to Max. "Soup for your dad. On the house."

"Wow," said Warren. "Hey, do you have any poster paint?"

"Just toothpicks and soup today."

"Toothpicks and soup are great," said Max. "Thank you!" His happy, wanting-to-run feeling was back, but running would spill the soup. Instead, Max and Warren quick-walked out to the sidewalk, where Ms. Tibbet and the dogs were waiting.

"Excellent work, young heroes," said Ms. Tibbet.

"Wumph," said Peggoty, bumping the soup bag with her nose.

By the time they returned to Dad's apartment building, there were check marks next to every item on the quest list except for one.

They had collected pebbles off the sidewalk. The Birch Street Produce man had given them some kale to use for shrubs and leaves. At the park, they gathered small rocks and strong sticks that would make good trees—

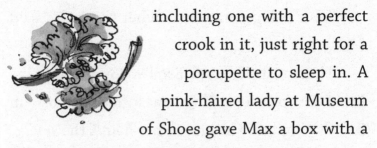 including one with a perfect crook in it, just right for a porcupette to sleep in. A pink-haired lady at Museum of Shoes gave Max a box with a picture of a high-heeled sandal on the side.

But they still did not have paints.

"I am sorry, young hero, that we did not acquire everything on your quest list," said Ms. Tibbet as they rode the elevator to the second floor. "But I hope you feel better than you did before."

"I guess so," said Max. He knew he should be happy about all the things they had found. But without paint, the shoebox would still have a sandal picture on it and the toothpicks would still look like toothpicks. His habitat would not look right at all. The porcupine was a great mammal. It deserved a great habitat.

The elevator doors opened. Estelle was in the hallway again. She was no longer covered in yellow, but her one-armed baby doll, Monica, was.

"Your doll got mustard on her too, huh?" said Max.

"Not mustard," said Estelle. "Sunshine." She lifted the doll's foot. There was a green sploosh on it. "That's grass. The blue in her hair is the sky."

Max looked at Warren. Warren looked at Max. "Paints!" they said at the very same time.

Mr. Polaski was very happy to let Max use Estelle's paints for his project. "I have had all the sunshine I need for a while," he said.

It took several knocks before Dad opened the apartment door. He looked like he had just woken up. His eyes were pillowy and his hair stuck up in all directions.

"Like quills upon a fretful porcupine," said Ms. Tibbet. "Fitting." She bowed her head at Max and

Warren. "Our quest is concluded. You have been brave and clever and persistent. Well done, young heroes."

"Well done to you, too, elderly sage," said Warren.

"Warren," said Dad. "I don't think—"

Ms. Tibbet held up her hand. "All is well, L. LeRoy."

Max bowed to Ms. Tibbet. "Thanks for your help."

"It was my pleasure. I have not been on a quest

in a very long time." Ms. Tibbet handed Dad his bag of soup. "And now, by your leave, I shall return these beasts to their lair. Fare thee well, young heroes!"

"Fare thee well!" said Max.

CHAPTER

FIVE

Warren barely got his beaver dam glued together before his mom came to pick him up. He left his Super Sticky Glue behind for Max to use.

"Fare thee well, Max," he said.

"Fare thee well, Warren," said Max. "See you Monday."

After Warren left, it was just Max and Dad in the apartment. "You can go back to bed if you want," said Max.

"I got a great nap while you were on your quest," said Dad. He sat down at the breakfast bar next to Max. "Would you show me what you're working on?"

Max shook his head. "I don't like it."

The entire time that Warren had been gluing, Max had been arranging and rearranging his quest items, but nothing looked right. If he rested the box on the long side, the stick trees were too tall. If he set the box on the short side, the trees fit, but there was no room to build a den.

"This box is too small," Max said.

"The box is the problem?" asked Dad. "Max, I may not have paints or Super Sticky Glue, but I am the King of Boxes. Follow me. And bring your things."

Max followed Dad into his bedroom. How could he have forgotten? Dad's room was filled with boxes!

Dad opened a cube-shaped box and turned

it over on the bed. Blankets and sheets tumbled out. "How about this one?" asked Dad. "It's roomy."

Max considered the box. "Too roomy. My habitat would be mostly sky, and I don't have that much blue paint."

"How about this one?" Dad opened another box. It was filled with bathroom things like soap and aspirin bottles and extra shampoo. Dad put the things in the bathroom cupboards while Max examined the box. It was a rectangle, but it was still too big. Plus, it smelled like coconut shaving cream. Porcupine habitat should not smell like shaving cream.

The third box Dad opened was very heavy. When he turned it over on the bed, pots and pans clonked out. "I didn't know I had pots and pans," said Dad. "Your grandma must have packed this one." He took the pots and pans into the kitchen.

The pots-and-pans box was too big, too. All of the boxes were too big.

"Hmm . . ." Dad made his really-thinking-hard-about-something sound. "Tell me more about porcupine habitat."

Max explained about the forest floor and how

he wanted to show a little porcupine den and lots of trees, including the one with the crooked branch for a porcupette to sleep in.

"Hmm . . . I wonder . . ." Dad left the room and came back with Friday night's pizza box. "What would you think of something like this?" He folded the lid of the box in half so that the back part closed flat like it normally would, but the front part stuck straight up.

"So, underneath the closed part could be the den," said Max. "And I could paint a forest scene on the sticking-up part!"

"We'll have to tape the top part open," said Dad. "Luckily, in addition to being the King of Boxes, I have a side gig as the Prince of Packing Tape."

Dad held the lid in position while Max taped it in place. "Thanks," said Max. "But I have to do the rest by myself, otherwise it won't be *my* habitat project."

"That sounds right." Dad spread packing paper on the floor and set the pizza box on top of it. "Let me know if you need help, okay?"

"Okay," said Max. "You can go back to sleep if you want."

"Thank you. But right now I have a habitat project of my own to finish."

Max arranged and glued and taped and

painted. Dad opened boxes and put the old things he found in all the new places they belonged. They both worked so hard that they did not notice the sky growing darker outside. Finally, Dad clicked on the bedroom light.

"Well, what do you think?" asked Dad.

Max looked up from his project and around at Dad's room. It was amazing. The room was bright and clean and there were no boxes in it, except for the one Dad was using as a nightstand.

"I guess you're not the King of Boxes anymore," said Max.

"Guess not," said Dad. "Now I'm just a guy who has finally moved into his apartment."

Max could not tell if Dad was happy about not being King anymore. His voice sounded sort of creaky—but maybe that was just his not-cold?

"It's a very nice habitat," said Max.

Dad smiled. "Thanks, sport."

"I'm not a sport. I'm a porcupine expert." Max

put down his paintbrush. His porcupine habitat looked great. He had filled in some of the den with rocks and pebbles so a porcupette could feel snug and safe. The trees were all glued in place with

Warren's Super Sticky Glue. He had painted the toothpick sticks and glued in the kale bushes very realistically. His forest background was the best of all. Max had painted the bottom part with greens and browns and put blue sky above it. Once that was dry, he painted lots of tall brown lines, so it looked like a whole forest of trees. He had done it patiently, one line at a time, just like he had drawn the quills on the porcupine on the cover of his report.

"Great job, pal," said Dad. "But where's the porcupine?"

"On the bench at school," said Max. "Mom and I made it. It's really good."

"Your mom is very good with art projects," said Dad.

"I know," said Max. "And you are very good with pizza boxes."

"Speaking of which," said Dad. "I need to order another. Should we get a pizza to go with it?"

"Yes," said Max. "Cheese and pepperoni."

Max admired his habitat again. On Monday, he would add his clay porcupine and then it would be perfect. Almost. "If I had more clay," he said, once Dad got off the phone with the pizza guy, "I'd make some porcupettes."

"Hmm." Dad was thinking again. "I don't have clay, but I do have the Internet." He flipped open his laptop and searched for a recipe for air-drying dough. "Bingo!" said Dad. "Don't tell Grandma that the first thing I cooked with her pots and pantry supplies was porcupine clay."

When the dough was ready, Max made two small porcupettes with cut-up ukulele strings for quills. He shaped one to fit in the den and the other to rest in the crook of the tree. Dad watched the whole time.

"If you were a porcupette, which do you think you'd like better? Sleeping in a den or sleeping in a tree?" asked Dad.

Max thought about it. A den would be cozy and dark and warm, and a tree would be bright

and breezy and you could see a long, long way.

"I think porcupettes like both," said Max. "Some days are den days and some days are tree days, but both are their habitat. Both are home."

Dad put his arm around Max. "You're a good boy, Max."

"I'm a young hero and a porcupine expert," said Max. "And a good boy too, I guess."

"I guess," said Dad. He pulled a tissue from his pocket and blew his nose.

"Are you crying, Dad?" asked Max.

"Crying? *Pfft!*" said Dad. "I just have a cold."

If Max knew how to raise his eyebrow like Mrs. Maloof, he would have.

"Should we clean up a little?" asked Dad.

Max nodded. "I'll put the habitat in my room," he said.

My room, thought Max. *My room. In our apartment.*

Just like a porcupine, he had two places to

sleep. Both were safe and both were good. Some days were house days and some days were apartment days.

But both were home.

Be sure to join Max on his next adventure in

$\mathbf{M}$ax is heading off on a road trip with Mom. With miles to travel, cousins to meet, and a tall roller-coaster to ride (maybe), it will be quite the experience! But Max always spends weekends with Dad; will Dad be okay if he's left behind? And will Max be brave enough for all the new explorations ahead of him?

PART ONE

The Announcement

CHAPTER
ONE

On Monday morning after breakfast, Mom made an announcement. "We are going on an adventure."

Max was surprised. Mom was not the sort of mom who made announcements about adventures. She was the sort of mom who made announcements about the laundry needing to be put away, or how proud she was of Max's report card, or that Max's hair was getting long and it was time for a trim.

"An adventure to the barbershop?" asked Max.

"A real adventure." Mom handed Max a card that said:

BIRTHDAY PARTY AND FAMILY REUNION

Beneath the words was a photo of a very, very old woman wearing a very, very old cowboy hat.

"Your Great-Great-Aunt Victory is turning one hundred years old."

Max was surprised at this, too. "I have a Great-Great-Aunt Victory?"

"You've met her before," said Mom. "When you were three."

Max looked closely at the photo. He did not

remember meeting any very, very old women in cowboy hats.

"You sat in her lap and sang the alphabet song into a soup spoon. It was adorable." Mom said "adorable" in a way that made Max feel like he was still only three years old instead of nine. "My uncles called you Spooner after that. You really don't remember?"

Max was glad he did not remember. Who wanted to remember being called Spooner?

Mom tapped the invitation. "Read the inside," she said.

VICTORY IS TURNING 100
Join us at her favorite spot
in the world,
Bronco Burt's Wild Ride
Amusement Park,
for a day of ropin', ridin',
and reminiscin'!

"Have I been to Bronco Burt's before, too?" asked Max.

"No," said Mom. "But I went dozens of times when I was growing up in Pennsylvania."

Max had seen Pennsylvania on the map in Mrs. Maloof's classroom. It didn't even touch Michigan. There was a whole Ohio between. "Pennsylvania is pretty far away."

"That is the best part," said Mom. "You and I are going on a road trip!"

Wow! A birthday party, an amusement park, and a road trip? This *did* sound like an adventure! "Will I get to miss school?" asked Max.

"The party is on Saturday. We'll drive to Pennsylvania after school on Friday and come back on Sunday night. You won't miss a thing," said Mom.

"Oh," said Max.

Mom laughed. "You look disappointed. Guess you really wanted to miss some school, huh?"

Max shook his head. He wouldn't have minded

missing a little school,
but that was not why
he was disappointed.
"I'd like to go with you,
but I can't."

"You can't?" asked
Mom. "Why not?"

Max got quieter. He
did not want Mom to

feel bad about her mistake, especially when she
sounded so happy. "You work at Shady Acres on
the weekends and I go to Dad's, remember?" The
schedule was right there on the family calendar,
in Mom's no-budge, no-smudge ink. "You only
get me on the weekdays."

"That's usually true. But your Great-Great-
Aunt Victory will turn one hundred only once.
I've talked to your dad and he said if you want to
go to the party, you should go. You do want to go,
don't you?"

Max did want to go, but he wished he didn't have to leave Dad alone on the weekend. Ever since Dad had gotten his apartment, he and Max had spent the weekends together. They ate pizza and watched movies and walked Ms. Tibbet's basset hounds and had breakfast at Ace's Coffee Shop every morning. What would Dad do without Max to keep him company?

"Oh, Max, you're going to love it," Mom continued. "Bronco Burt's has rides and barbecue stands and a Wild West arcade and . . ." Her face turned dreamy, like it did when she took a bite of her favorite Mocha Monkey ice cream. ". . . the Big Buckaroo."

The Big Buckaroo? Who was the Big Buckaroo?

He sounded to Max like some kind of movie-star guy. Since when did Mom care about movie-star guys?

"I have to get to the bus stop," said Max.

Mom looked at the clock. "We still have a few minutes. Don't you want to talk more about our trip?"

"I don't want to be late." Max grabbed his backpack. He ran all the way to his bus stop. And then, because he was early, he ran down the block and back as many times as he could before the bus came.